EMERGE: A SYMPHONY OF RESILIENCE

Gloria L. Foster

GLOBAL
PUBLISHING
SOLUTIONS

EMERGE: A SYMPHONY OF RESILIENCE by Gloria L. Foster

Published by Global Publishing Solutions, LLC
923 Fieldside Drive
Matteson, Illinois 60443
www.globalpublishingsolutions.com

Library of Congress Control Number: 2024943335

International Standard Book Number: 979-8-9900270-2-2

E-book International Standard Book Number: 979-8-9900270-8-4

Printed in the United States of America

TABLE OF CONTENTS

INTRODUCTION

In the enchanting town of Sommerville, where the echoes of the past intertwine with the promise of the future, a new chapter is about to unfold. "Echoes of Resilience" invites you to embark on a journey of courage, community, and the unwavering power of hope.

As we reunite with familiar faces and discover new stories waiting to be told, we are reminded that Sommerville is more than just a place—it is a beacon of resilience in a world filled with uncertainty. From the bustling main street to the tranquil countryside, every corner of this beloved town holds a tale of triumph and transformation.

Join Jonathan, Sheila, Xavier, and a host of other vibrant characters as they navigate the challenges of life, love, and loss, guided by the bonds of friendship and the strength of their shared convictions. From uncovering long-buried secrets to weathering the fiercest of storms, they will face every obstacle with unwavering resolve, knowing that together, they are stronger than they could ever be alone.

As the sun sets on one chapter and rises on the next, "Echoes of Resilience" reminds us that even in our darkest moments, the echoes of hope and courage can light the way forward. So, dear reader, let us turn the page and discover the stories that await us in the heartwarming pages of Sommerville's latest tale.

CHAPTER 1: A REUNION OF SOULS

The sun dipped low on the horizon, casting long shadows across the streets of Sommerville as Jonathan made his way to Mary's house. It had been years since he had seen his old friend, and he was eager to catch up and share his plans for making a difference in their community.

As he approached the familiar picket fence that surrounded Mary's front yard, Jonathan felt a sense of warmth and familiarity wash over him. The memories of their childhood flooded back—playing tag in the backyard, sharing secrets under the old oak tree, dreaming of the future they would build together.

Mary greeted him with a warm smile as she opened the door, her eyes bright with excitement. "Jonathan, it's been too long! Come in, come in."

Jonathan stepped inside, the scent of home-cooked meals and freshly baked cookies filling the air. It felt good to be back in Mary's cozy kitchen, surrounded by the comforting embrace of friendship and shared history.

As they settled into their chairs, Jonathan couldn't help but feel a surge of gratitude for the bond they shared. Mary had always been there for him, a steadfast pillar of support and encouragement, and he knew that he could count on her to stand by his side as he embarked on this new chapter of his life.

Over cups of steaming tea, Jonathan shared his vision for creating change in Sommerville—a community-driven movement focused on addressing the root causes of violence and inequality. He spoke passionately about the need to invest in education, provide job opportunities for at-risk youth, and dismantle the systems of oppression that held their community back.

Mary listened intently, her eyes shining with pride and admiration. "Jonathan, I'm so proud of you," she said, her voice tinged with emotion. "You've always had a heart for justice, and it's inspiring to see you taking action to make a difference."

Jonathan smiled gratefully, touched by Mary's words. "Thank you, Mary. But I couldn't do it without your support. You've always been my rock, my guiding light in times of darkness."

Their conversation turned to memories of their shared past—the highs and lows, the triumphs and tribulations. They laughed about their misadventures in high school, reminisced about their dreams of changing the world, and marveled at how far they had come since those carefree days of youth.

But amidst the laughter and nostalgia, there was also a sense of solemnity—a recognition of the challenges that lay ahead and the responsibility they bore to their community. They knew that the road ahead would be difficult, but they were determined to face it together, united in their commitment to creating a better future for Sommerville.

As the evening drew to a close, Jonathan and Mary shared a heartfelt embrace, their bond stronger than ever. They knew that their reunion was more than just a chance to catch up—it was a reaffirmation of their shared values, their shared dreams, and their shared mission to leave the world a little better than they found it.

CHAPTER 2: ECHOES OF THE PAST

The gentle hum of cicadas filled the air as Xavier stepped out onto the porch of his childhood home. Sommerville had always held a special place in his heart, a tapestry of memories woven with laughter, tears, and the bittersweet symphony of life.

As he gazed out at the familiar sights—the towering oak trees, the quaint houses with their colorful shutters, the bustling streets alive with the rhythm of everyday life—Xavier felt a surge of nostalgia wash over him. It had been years since he had returned to his hometown, and yet, it felt as though he had never left.

Taking a deep breath, Xavier let the memories flood back, transporting him to a time long gone but forever etched in his soul. He remembered the carefree days of his youth, spent exploring the woods with his friends, playing basketball at the local court, and dreaming of a future filled with endless possibilities.

But amidst the nostalgia, there was also a sense of longing—a yearning for connection, for belonging, for the comfort of familiar faces and shared experiences. Xavier knew that he had grown and changed since leaving Sommerville, but a part of him would always remain rooted in the soil of his hometown, forever bound to its essence.

Lost in thought, Xavier was startled by the sound of footsteps behind him. Turning around, he saw a figure emerging from the shadows—a familiar face framed by the golden light of the setting sun.

"Tobias?" Xavier exclaimed, his voice tinged with disbelief. "Is that really you?"

Tobias smiled warmly, his eyes crinkling at the corners with genuine affection. "It's me, old friend," he said, his voice a soft echo of the past. "It's been too long."

Embracing each other like long-lost brothers, Xavier and Tobias shared a moment of quiet camaraderie, their bond unbroken by time or distance. They had been through so much together—the highs and lows, the triumphs and tribulations—and yet, their friendship had endured, a testament to the enduring power of connection.

As they settled into the comfortable silence of shared memories, Xavier felt a sense of peace wash over him. Sommerville may have changed over the years, but the essence of the town remained unchanged—a sanctuary of warmth and belonging, a haven for the soul weary traveler.

With a renewed sense of gratitude for the ties that bound them together, Xavier and Tobias set out to explore the town they once called home, eager to rediscover its hidden treasures and forge new memories that would last a lifetime.

CHAPTER 3: EMBRACING THE UNKNOWN

The morning sun cast a golden glow over Sommerville, bathing the town in a warm embrace as its residents went about their daily routines. Sheila stepped out onto the porch of her childhood home, taking in the familiar sights and sounds of the sleepy town awakening to a new day.

Today was a day of beginnings—a chance to breathe new life into old dreams and forge a path forward guided by the wisdom of the past. With a sense of purpose, Sheila set out to reconnect with the community she had left behind, eager to learn from its triumphs and tribulations and lend her hand to the task of building a brighter future.

Her first stop was the local diner, a bustling hub of activity where townsfolk gathered to swap stories and share a hearty meal. As Sheila stepped through the door, she was greeted by the comforting aroma of freshly brewed coffee and the cheerful chatter of familiar faces.

"Morning, Sheila!" called out Mrs. Jenkins, the diner's owner, her smile as warm as the morning sun. "It's been too long, my dear. Come, sit down and tell me all about your adventures out there in the big wide world."

Settling into a booth by the window, Sheila found herself surrounded by old friends and neighbors, each eager to catch up on lost time and share their hopes and dreams for the future. As she listened to their stories of resilience and renewal, Sheila felt a sense of kinship and camaraderie that filled her heart with joy.

Over plates of fluffy pancakes and steaming cups of coffee, Sheila and her fellow townsfolk delved into discussions about the challenges facing Sommerville and the opportunities for positive change that lay ahead. From revitalizing the local economy to preserving the town's rich cultural heritage, there was no shortage of ideas and enthusiasm for making Sommerville an even better place to call home.

As the morning wore on and the diner filled with laughter and conversation, Sheila felt a renewed sense of purpose wash over her—a deep-seated conviction that together, the people of Sommerville could overcome any obstacle and achieve their shared vision of a brighter future.

Leaving the diner with a heart full of hope and determination, Sheila set out to explore the town she once called home, eager to immerse herself in its vibrant tapestry of history and tradition. From the historic main street lined with quaint shops and cafes to the tranquil beauty of the surrounding countryside, Sommerville held a treasure trove of memories waiting to be rediscovered.

As she wandered through the streets, Sheila found herself drawn to the old community center—the beating heart of Sommerville, where generations of residents had come together to celebrate, commiserate, and support one another through life's ups and downs.

Stepping through the door, Sheila was greeted by the sight of a group of children engaged in a lively game of tag, their laughter echoing off the walls as they raced around the room with boundless energy and enthusiasm. It was a scene straight out of her own childhood—a reminder of the timeless spirit of community that had always defined Sommerville.

As she watched the children play, Sheila felt a sense of optimism wash over her—a quiet reassurance that no matter where life took her, Sommerville would always be her home. In the laughter of its children and the warmth of its people, she found solace and strength—a reminder that the bonds of community were stronger than any challenge they might face.

With a smile on her face and a renewed sense of purpose in her heart, Sheila knew that her journey was just beginning. In Sommerville, amidst the echoes of change and the promise of tomorrow, she had found her place in the world—a place where dreams took root and flourished, and where the ties that bound them together would endure

for generations to come.

CHAPTER 4: WHISPERS OF THE PAST

As the sun dipped below the horizon, casting a soft orange glow over Sommerville, Sheila found herself drawn to the quiet solitude of the town's cemetery. It was a place steeped in history and memory—a sacred ground where the past and present converged in a timeless dance of remembrance.

Walking among the weathered gravestones, Sheila felt a sense of reverence wash over her—a deep appreciation for the lives that had shaped the town she loved and the stories that had woven its rich tapestry of heritage and tradition.

Stopping before a particularly weathered marker, Sheila knelt down, gently brushing away the fallen leaves to reveal the name etched into the stone: Margaret Thompson, beloved mother, cherished friend. It was a name Sheila had not spoken in years, yet its echoes lingered still, whispering of a bond that transcended time and space.

Closing her eyes, Sheila allowed herself to be transported back to a time long ago—a time when she and Margaret had walked these same hallowed grounds, their laughter mingling with the rustle of leaves and the soft murmur of the wind.

Memories flooded Sheila's mind like a river rushing downstream, carrying her back to a simpler time when life was filled with possibility and promise. She remembered the warmth of Margaret's smile, the kindness in her eyes, and the unwavering love that had sustained them through even the darkest of days.

As she knelt there in silent contemplation, Sheila felt a profound sense of gratitude welling up within her—a gratitude for the gift of Margaret's presence in her life and the countless lessons she had imparted along the way.

In that sacred moment, amidst the whispers of the past and the gentle embrace of the present, Sheila found solace and strength—a reminder that even in the face of loss and uncertainty, love endured, casting its light upon the darkest of shadows and guiding them toward the promise of a new dawn.

With a heart full of reverence and gratitude, Sheila rose to her feet, her spirit buoyed by the knowledge that Margaret's legacy lived on in the hearts of all who had been touched by her grace and compassion.

Turning to leave the cemetery behind, Sheila felt a renewed sense of purpose coursing through her veins—a quiet determination to honor Margaret's memory by embracing life's challenges with courage and resilience, and by forging ahead on the journey of self-discovery and growth.

As she made her way back to the town center, Sheila knew that the road ahead would not be easy, but she faced it with a newfound sense of clarity and conviction, buoyed by the memories of those who had gone before and the unwavering support of the community she held dear.

With each step she took, Sheila felt the whispers of the past guiding her forward, urging her to embrace the future with open arms and a steadfast resolve to make the most of every precious moment she was given. And as she looked ahead to the dawn of a new day, Sheila knew that she was ready to face whatever challenges lay ahead, secure in the knowledge that she was never truly alone.

CHAPTER 5: ECHOES OF CHANGE

The morning sun cast a warm glow over Sommerville as Jonathan stepped out onto the quaint main street. The familiar sights and sounds of his hometown greeted him—a comforting reminder of the ties that bound him to this place, even after all these years.

As he strolled along the bustling thoroughfare, Jonathan couldn't help but marvel at the changes that had taken root in Sommerville since his return. The once-sleepy town had undergone a remarkable transformation, blossoming into a vibrant community teeming with life and vitality.

Gazing up at the newly renovated storefronts and bustling cafes that lined the street, Jonathan felt a swell of pride in his chest. It was a testament to the resilience and determination of the people of Sommerville—a testament to their unwavering commitment to building a brighter future for themselves and generations to come.

Lost in thought, Jonathan nearly collided with Xavier, who was standing outside a charming bookstore, a wide grin spread across his face.

"Hey there, Jonathan! Fancy running into you here," Xavier exclaimed, clapping his old friend on the back.

Jonathan chuckled, shaking his head in amusement. "I could say the same to you, Xavier. What brings you to this neck of the woods?"

Xavier gestured toward the bookstore with a flourish. "Just doing a bit of browsing, you know. I heard they have a great selection of mystery novels, and you know how much I love a good whodunit."

Jonathan grinned, a spark of mischief dancing in his eyes. "Ah, so you're still chasing after those elusive clues, huh? Some things never change."

Xavier laughed, his eyes twinkling with mirth. "You got that right, my friend. But enough about me—what brings you back to Sommerville? Last I heard, you were knee-deep in some high-profile case down in the city."

Jonathan's expression grew solemn as he recounted the details of the case he had been working on—the twists and turns, the highs and lows, and the relentless pursuit of justice that had driven him forward.

"It sounds like quite the ordeal," Xavier remarked, his tone sympathetic. "But knowing you, Jonathan, I have no doubt that you gave it your all."

Jonathan nodded, a sense of resolve settling over him. "I did what I could, Xavier. But sometimes, the fight for justice takes more than just one person—it takes a community, united in purpose and driven by a shared vision of a better world."

Xavier regarded his friend with a thoughtful expression. "You know, Jonathan, you're absolutely right. And speaking of community, have you had a chance to catch up with Sheila since you've been back?"

Jonathan's eyes lit up at the mention of Sheila's name, memories of their shared adventures flooding his mind. "Not yet, but I was hoping to swing by her place later this afternoon. It's been far too long since we last caught up."

Xavier nodded, a knowing smile playing at the corners of his lips. "Well, you'll be pleased to know that Sheila has been hard at work spearheading some pretty impressive initiatives here in Sommerville. I have a feeling you two will have plenty to talk about."

Jonathan's curiosity was piqued. "Oh? Do tell, Xavier. What's Sheila been up to?"

Xavier leaned in closer, his voice lowered to a conspiratorial whisper. "Let's just say she's been channeling her inner activist, rallying the troops and championing causes left and right. You'll have to see it for yourself to believe it."

A sense of excitement bubbled up inside Jonathan as he listened to Xavier's words. It was clear that Sommerville was in the midst of a profound transformation—a transformation driven by the collective efforts of its passionate residents, each one committed to making a difference in their own unique way.

As he bid farewell to Xavier and continued on his way, Jonathan couldn't help but feel a renewed sense of purpose coursing through his veins. Sommerville may have been his hometown, but it was also a place of new beginnings— a place where he could join forces with old friends and new allies alike to shape a future defined by hope, resilience, and the unwavering belief in the power of community.

With each step he took, Jonathan felt the echoes of change reverberating through the streets of Sommerville, urging him forward on the journey that lay ahead. And as he looked toward the horizon, he knew that the best was yet to come.

CHAPTER 6: UNVEILING THE TRUTH

The days blurred into nights as Jonathan and his friends delved deeper into the heart of the mystery gripping Sommerville. With each passing hour, the tension in the air grew thicker, suffocating the once-peaceful town in a blanket of fear and uncertainty.

Determined to uncover the truth, Jonathan had spent countless hours poring over evidence, following leads, and piecing together the fragments of information scattered throughout the community. But despite his best efforts, the identity of the shadowy figure remained elusive, lurking just beyond his grasp.

Frustration gnawed at Jonathan's insides as he paced the length of his small office, the dim light of the desk lamp casting long shadows on the walls. He couldn't shake the feeling that they were missing something—some crucial piece of the puzzle that would unravel the mystery once and for all.

As if on cue, a knock echoed through the room, pulling Jonathan from his thoughts. He crossed the floor in a few quick strides and pulled open the door, revealing Sheila standing in the hallway, her expression grave.

"We need to talk, Jonathan," Sheila said, her voice low and urgent.

Jonathan's heart sank as he took in the look on her face. Whatever news she had to share, he knew it wouldn't be good.

Sheila stepped into the office, closing the door behind her with a soft click. She took a deep breath, her eyes fixed on Jonathan's.

"I've been doing some digging of my own," Sheila began, her voice barely above a whisper. "And I think I may have stumbled onto something—something big."

Jonathan's interest piqued at her words. "What do you mean, Sheila? What did you find?"

Sheila hesitated for a moment, as if gathering her thoughts. "I've been looking into the recent string of incidents—the petty crimes, the unrest in the neighborhoods—and I noticed a pattern. A pattern that led me to one person: Tristan Brooks."

Jonathan's brow furrowed in confusion. "Tristan Brooks? Who is he?"

Sheila took a deep breath, steeling herself for what she was about to reveal. "He's an old acquaintance of mine from high school. He left Sommerville years ago, but it seems he's returned—and not for the best of reasons."

Jonathan's mind raced as he processed Sheila's words. Tristan Brooks—a name he hadn't heard in years, yet one that sent a chill down his spine. If Sheila was right, then Marcus Tristan could be the key to unlocking the mystery that had consumed their town.

"Where can we find him?" Jonathan asked, his voice tinged with determination.

Sheila hesitated for a moment before responding. "I'm not sure, but I have a feeling he's been hiding out at the old abandoned warehouse on the outskirts of town. It's worth checking out."

Jonathan nodded, his mind already racing ahead to the next steps. "Alright, let's gather the others and head over there. We need to confront Tristan and get to the bottom of this once and for all."

With a renewed sense of purpose, Jonathan and Sheila left the office, their footsteps echoing down the empty hallway. Outside, the night air hung heavy with anticipation, the promise of resolution lingering just beyond the horizon.

As they made their way through the darkened streets of Sommerville, Jonathan couldn't shake the feeling that they were on the verge of a breakthrough—that the truth they sought was within their grasp, waiting to be unveiled in the shadows of the old abandoned warehouse.

With each step they took, the weight of the mystery pressing down upon them, Jonathan and Sheila braced themselves for the confrontation that awaited, knowing that their journey was far from over.

But deep down, they also knew that no matter what lay ahead, they would face it together, united in their commitment to bringing justice to their town and peace to their community once more.

CHAPTER 7: THE LIGHT OF HOPE

The old, abandoned warehouse loomed before them, a silent sentinel guarding its secrets in the heart of the night. Jonathan and Sheila stood at the entrance, their hearts pounding in their chests as they prepared to confront the darkness that lay within.

With a silent nod, Jonathan pushed open the creaking door, the rusty hinges groaning in protest as they swung open to reveal the dimly lit interior of the warehouse. The air was thick with dust and decay, the only sound the echoing drip of water from a leaky pipe overhead.

Cautiously, Jonathan and Sheila stepped inside, their eyes scanning the shadows for any sign of movement. As they made their way deeper into the belly of the warehouse, a sense of foreboding settled over them, the weight of the unknown pressing down upon their shoulders like a leaden shroud.

But despite the darkness that surrounded them, Jonathan and Sheila pressed on, their resolve unwavering in the face of adversity. They knew that they were close—close to uncovering the truth that had eluded them for so long, close to bringing an end to the mystery that had gripped Sommerville in its icy grasp.

Suddenly, a voice echoed through the darkness, sending shivers down Jonathan's spine.

"Well, well, well. What do we have here?"

Jonathan and Sheila spun around to find Tristan Brooks emerging from the shadows, his face twisted into a malicious grin. He was flanked by a group of shadowy figures, their eyes gleaming with malice as they closed in on their prey.

"Tristan," Jonathan said, his voice steady despite the adrenaline coursing through his veins. "We know what you've been up to. It's time to come clean."

Tristan chuckled darkly, his eyes flashing with contempt. "And why would I do that, Jonathan? What's in it for me?"

Jonathan took a step forward, his gaze unwavering. "Justice, Tristan. For the people of Sommerville. For the community you've hurt with your actions."

Tristan sneered, a cold glint in his eyes. "You think you can stop me, Jonathan? You and your ragtag band of do-gooders? You're nothing but a thorn in my side—a nuisance to be dealt with."

Before Jonathan could respond, Tristan signaled to his cohorts, and suddenly, the warehouse was alive with movement as they closed in on Jonathan and Sheila, their intentions clear.

But Jonathan refused to back down—not now, not ever. With a fierce determination burning in his chest, he raised his voice above the chaos, calling out to his friends and allies for help.

And in that moment, as the shadows closed in around them and the echoes of their struggle reverberated through the darkness, Jonathan knew that no matter what trials lay ahead, they would face them together, united in their commitment to bringing light to the darkest corners of Sommerville and hope to those who needed it most.

For in the end, it was the light of hope that would guide them forward, illuminating the path to a future defined by justice, compassion, and the unwavering belief in the power of community.

And as the first rays of dawn broke through the clouds, bathing Sommerville in a golden glow, Jonathan and his friends stood tall amidst the wreckage of the old abandoned warehouse, their spirits unbroken, their resolve unwavering, and their hearts filled with the promise of a new beginning.

CHAPTER 8: A NEW VOICE

Naomi Anders sat at the head of a long, polished table in the conference room, her heart pounding in her chest. Around her, colleagues and acquaintances mingled, chatting animatedly about their plans and aspirations. Naomi had been invited to this meeting to discuss her latest project—a community outreach program aimed at supporting at-risk youth in Sommerville. But today, she felt an overwhelming sense of unease.

As she tried to follow the conversation, Naomi's thoughts drifted to her strained relationships with her family and friends. They had always seen her as the black sheep, the one who could never quite fit in. Lately, these tensions had reached a breaking point, and the pressure was taking a toll on her mental and physical health.

"Naomi, what do you think?" someone asked, jolting her back to the present.

She opened her mouth to respond but found her words coming out in a slurred, incoherent mess. Her vision blurred, and a strange numbness crept up one side of her body. Panic set in as she realized she was having a stroke. She needed help, but the people around her continued their conversations, oblivious to her distress.

Desperately, Naomi reached for her cellphone, but one of her colleagues, Rebecca, took it from her hand. "Let's focus on the meeting," she said dismissively, placing the phone out of Naomi's reach. Another colleague, Mark, casually slid her purse away from her as well.

Helpless and terrified, Naomi struggled to speak, to make them understand. But her efforts were in vain. The room seemed to spin around her as she fought to stay conscious.

Summoning all her strength, Naomi managed to push herself up from her chair. She stumbled toward the door, each step a monumental effort. As she reached the exit, she caught the eye of her co-worker, Eric.

"I think Naomi's having a stroke," Eric said, his voice lacking urgency. "I'll call 911."

But he didn't move. Naomi's heart sank as she realized he wasn't going to help. Driven by sheer willpower, she forced herself out the door and into the street.

She staggered down the sidewalk, each breath labored and painful. Her vision narrowed, and she felt herself slipping away. Just as she thought she could go no further, she saw a group of people gathered by the lake.

A woman in the group noticed her and exclaimed, "Oh my God, she's having a stroke!"

But no one moved to help. They stared at her with a mix of curiosity and concern, but none of them took action.

Feeling her strength waning, Naomi pushed on, driven by the primal need to survive. Her legs buckled, and she collapsed to the ground, darkness overtaking her.

CHAPTER 9: THE DAWN OF REALIZATION

Naomi awoke to the steady beeping of medical equipment and the sterile scent of a hospital room. Her eyes fluttered open, and she took in her surroundings—white walls, a curtain, and the soft hum of machines. She was alive, but barely.

A nurse entered the room, noticing that Naomi was awake. "Welcome back," she said gently. "You've been through quite an ordeal."

Naomi tried to speak, but her voice was weak, and her words came out slurred. The nurse seemed to understand her struggle.

"Don't try to talk just yet. You've had a stroke, but you're in good hands now. We'll take care of you."

Tears welled up in Naomi's eyes as the weight of her situation sank in. She had survived, but the journey ahead would be long and arduous. She thought of her family and friends, wondering if they even knew what had happened to her.

Days passed in a blur of medical procedures and physical therapy sessions. Slowly, Naomi regained some of her strength and clarity. Her speech improved, and she was able to communicate with the medical staff.

One afternoon, as she sat in her hospital bed, there was a knock on the door. It was Sheila, one of the key figures in Sommerville's community efforts.

"Naomi," Sheila said, her voice filled with concern. "I just heard what happened. I'm so sorry. How are you feeling?"

Naomi managed a weak smile. "Better, thanks. It's been rough."

Sheila sat down beside her, taking her hand. "I can't believe no one helped you. It's horrifying. But you're strong, and you're going to get through this."

Naomi nodded, tears spilling down her cheeks. "I felt so alone, Sheila. I thought I was going to die."

"You're not alone," Sheila reassured her. "You have us, the community, and we're going to support you every step of the way."

CHAPTER 10: NEW BEGINNINGS

Weeks turned into months as Naomi continued her recovery. She worked tirelessly in physical therapy, determined to regain her strength and independence. Her relationships with her family and friends remained strained, but she found solace in the support of her new allies in Sommerville.

Sheila and Jonathan visited regularly, offering their encouragement and assistance. They helped her navigate the healthcare system, provided emotional support, and even organized a community fundraiser to help cover her medical expenses.

One sunny afternoon, as Naomi walked slowly around the hospital garden with the aid of a cane, she felt a sense of renewal. She had faced death and come out the other side, stronger and more resilient than ever.

"Naomi," Sheila said, walking beside her. "When you're ready, we could really use your help with the community outreach program. Your experience and strength would be an inspiration to so many."

Naomi smiled, feeling a spark of hope ignite within her. "I'd like that, Sheila. I want to make a difference, just like you and Jonathan."

And so, Naomi embarked on a new chapter of her life. She found purpose in helping others, turning her pain into a source of strength and resilience. With the support of her friends and community, she discovered that even in the darkest moments, there was always a glimmer of hope, a chance for new beginnings

CHAPTER 11: EMBRACING THE UNKNOWN

The morning sun cast a golden glow over Sommerville, bathing the town in a warm embrace as its residents went about their daily routines. Sheila stepped out onto the porch of her childhood home, taking in the familiar sights and sounds of the sleepy town awakening to a new day.

Today was a day of beginnings—a chance to breathe new life into old dreams and forge a path forward guided by the wisdom of the past. With a sense of purpose, Sheila set out to reconnect with the community she had left behind, eager to learn from its triumphs and tribulations and lend her hand to the task of building a brighter future.

Her first stop was the local diner, a bustling hub of activity where townsfolk gathered to swap stories and share a hearty meal. As Sheila stepped through the door, she was greeted by the comforting aroma of freshly brewed coffee and the cheerful chatter of familiar faces.

"Morning, Sheila!" called out Mrs. Jenkins, the diner's owner, her smile as warm as the morning sun. "It's been too long, my dear. Come, sit down and tell me all about your adventures out there in the big wide world."

Settling into a booth by the window, Sheila found herself surrounded by old friends and neighbors, each eager to catch up on lost time and share their hopes and dreams for the future. As she listened to their stories of resilience and renewal, Sheila felt a sense of kinship and camaraderie that filled her heart with joy.

Over plates of fluffy pancakes and steaming cups of coffee, Sheila and her fellow townsfolk delved into discussions about the challenges facing Sommerville and the opportunities for positive change that lay ahead. From revitalizing the local economy to preserving the town's rich cultural heritage, there was no shortage of ideas and enthusiasm for making Sommerville an even better place to call home.

As the morning wore on and the diner filled with laughter and conversation, Sheila felt a renewed sense of purpose wash over her—a deep-seated conviction that together, the people of Sommerville could overcome any obstacle and achieve their shared vision of a brighter future.

Leaving the diner with a heart full of hope and determination, Sheila set out to explore the town she once called home, eager to immerse herself in its vibrant tapestry of history and tradition. From the historic main street lined with quaint shops and cafes to the tranquil beauty of the surrounding countryside, Sommerville held a treasure trove of memories waiting to be rediscovered.

As she wandered through the streets, Sheila found herself drawn to the old community center—the beating heart of Sommerville, where generations of residents had come together to celebrate, commiserate, and support one another through life's ups and downs.

Stepping through the door, Sheila was greeted by the sight of a group of children engaged in a lively game of tag, their laughter echoing off the walls as they raced around the room with boundless energy and enthusiasm. It was a scene straight out of her own childhood, a testament to the enduring spirit of community that had always defined Sommerville.

Moved by the sight, Sheila felt a renewed sense of determination to contribute to the community's efforts to create a brighter future for its residents. She knew that the road ahead would be challenging, but she was ready to face it with an open heart and a steadfast commitment to the values that had shaped her upbringing.

As the afternoon gave way to evening, Sheila found herself reflecting on the journey that had brought her back to Sommerville—the twists and turns, the triumphs and setbacks, and the lessons learned along the way. She knew that her story was just one of many, each thread weaving together to form the rich tapestry of life in their beloved town.

The wind had begun to pick up, the first signs of the approaching hurricane making their presence known. The townsfolk were preparing for the worst, boarding up windows and securing their homes against the impending storm. Sheila joined the effort, helping her neighbors and offering words of encouragement as they braced themselves for what was to come.

As the night fell and the storm began to rage, Sheila found herself surrounded by the comforting embrace of her community—a reminder that no matter what challenges lay ahead, they would face them together, united in their shared determination to create a better future for Sommerville.

CHAPTER 12: SHELTER FROM THE STORM

The wind howled with a ferocity that rattled the windows and sent shivers down the spines of Sommerville's residents. As the hurricane bore down on the town, families huddled together in their homes, seeking shelter from the storm that threatened to tear their world apart.

In the midst of the chaos, Jonathan, Xavier, and Sheila found themselves drawn to the community center—a beacon of hope and refuge in the face of adversity. As they arrived, they were greeted by the sight of familiar faces, each etched with a mix of fear and determination.

"Thank you for coming," said Mr. Thompson, the center's director, his voice steady despite the tension in the air. "We've set up emergency shelters for those who need it. Let's make sure everyone is safe and accounted for."

As the storm raged outside, the community center became a sanctuary—a place where neighbors came together to support one another and find solace in their shared humanity. Jonathan, Xavier, and Sheila joined the efforts, helping to distribute blankets and supplies, offering words of comfort, and lending a hand wherever it was needed.

Amidst the turmoil, they found moments of quiet reflection—glimpses of the resilience and strength that had always defined Sommerville. They listened to the stories of those who had weathered countless storms before, drawing inspiration from their courage and fortitude.

As the hours wore on, the storm showed no signs of abating. The wind howled and the rain pounded against the windows, but within the walls of the community center, there was a sense of solidarity and hope that could not be extinguished.

In the dim light of the shelter, Jonathan, Xavier, and Sheila found themselves drawn together, their shared commitment to their community stronger than ever. They knew that the road ahead would be challenging, but they were ready to face it with open hearts and unwavering determination.

"We'll get through this," Xavier said, his voice filled with conviction. "Together, we'll rebuild and come out stronger on the other side."

Sheila nodded, her eyes shining with resolve. "This is our home, and we'll do whatever it takes to protect it."

Jonathan placed a hand on their shoulders, a sense of calm washing over him. "We're not just survivors," he said softly. "We're a community. And together, we can overcome anything."

As the storm continued to rage outside, the people of Sommerville found strength in their unity, drawing on the bonds that had been forged through years of shared experiences and collective resilience. They knew that the journey ahead would be difficult, but they were ready to face it with courage and determination, guided by the light of their shared dreams and aspirations.

And as the first rays of dawn began to pierce the storm clouds, there was a sense of hope and renewal in the air— a promise of brighter days ahead, and a reminder that even in the darkest of times, the spirit of community would always shine through.

CHAPTER 13: RISING FROM THE ASHES

The aftermath of the hurricane left Sommerville a changed landscape, the once-familiar streets now littered with debris and the scars of the storm. But amidst the wreckage, there was also a sense of hope and determination—a resolve to rebuild and restore their beloved town to its former glory.

Jonathan, Xavier, and Sheila were at the forefront of the recovery efforts, working tirelessly to coordinate relief efforts and support their neighbors in the challenging days that followed. From organizing cleanup crews to distributing supplies and providing emotional support, they were a constant presence, their commitment to their community unwavering.

As they worked side by side with their fellow residents, they witnessed countless acts of kindness and generosity that spoke to the resilience and strength of the human spirit. Strangers became friends, and neighbors became family, united by a shared purpose and a common goal.

In the midst of the recovery efforts, Jonathan found himself reflecting on the journey that had brought him to this point—the struggles and setbacks, the moments of doubt and uncertainty, and the unwavering support of those who had stood by his side. He knew that the road ahead would be long and difficult, but he was ready to face it with a renewed sense of purpose and determination.

Xavier, too, found solace in the bonds that had been forged through the trials and tribulations of the past. As he worked alongside his friends and neighbors, he felt a deep sense of gratitude for the community that had shaped him and the people who had supported him through every challenge. He knew that together, they could overcome any obstacle and build a brighter future for Sommerville.

For Sheila, the recovery efforts were a reminder of the power of unity and collective action. As she helped to coordinate volunteer efforts and provide support to those in need, she felt a renewed sense of hope and optimism for the future. She knew that the journey ahead would be difficult, but she was ready to face it with an open heart and a steadfast commitment to the values that had always guided her.

As the weeks turned into months, the people of Sommerville began to rebuild their town, one step at a time. Homes were repaired, businesses reopened, and the familiar rhythm of everyday life slowly returned. But amidst the challenges, there was also a sense of renewal—a recognition that the storm had brought them closer together and strengthened the bonds that held their community together.

And as the first flowers of spring began to bloom, there was a sense of hope and possibility in the air—a reminder that even in the face of adversity, the spirit of community would always endure.

Jonathan, Xavier, and Sheila stood together on the steps of the community center, looking out at the town they had helped to rebuild. They knew that their journey was far from over, but they were ready to face whatever challenges lay ahead with courage and determination, guided by the light of their shared dreams and aspirations.

Together, they had weathered the storm and emerged stronger on the other side—a testament to the power of unity, resilience, and the enduring strength of the human spirit. And as they looked out at the town they called home, they knew that their journey was just beginning, and that the future held endless possibilities for growth, renewal, and hope.

CHAPTER 14: ALLIE'S AWAKENING

Allie stood at the edge of the forest, the canopy of trees casting dappled shadows on the ground below. She took a deep breath, the scent of pine and earth filling her senses as she prepared to embark on a journey of self-discovery.

For too long, Allie had felt adrift, unsure of her place in the world and the path she was meant to follow. But as she gazed into the depths of the forest, a sense of clarity washed over her—a deep-seated knowing that her destiny lay within its ancient embrace.

With a newfound sense of purpose burning in her chest, Allie stepped forward, the soft earth beneath her feet guiding her deeper into the heart of the forest. As she walked, she felt the weight of her doubts and fears begin to lift, replaced by a sense of peace and belonging that she had long yearned for.

With each step she took, Allie felt a connection to the natural world growing stronger—a recognition of the interconnectedness of all living things and the sacredness of the earth that sustained them. She marveled at the beauty of the world around her, from the gentle rustle of leaves in the breeze to the chorus of birdsong that filled the air.

As she journeyed deeper into the forest, Allie found herself drawn to a secluded glade bathed in soft sunlight. She closed her eyes and let the warmth wash over her, a sense of calm enveloping her like a comforting blanket.

In that moment, Allie felt a presence beside her—a whisper of ancient wisdom that stirred something deep within her soul. She opened her eyes and saw a figure standing before her, cloaked in robes of green and gold.

"Welcome, child," the figure said, their voice like the gentle rustle of leaves in the wind. "I have been expecting you."

Allie's heart fluttered with a mixture of awe and wonder as she gazed upon the figure before her. There was a familiarity in their presence—a sense of recognition that resonated deep within her being.

"I have watched you from afar, Allie," the figure continued, their gaze penetrating to the core of her being. "I have seen the struggles you have faced and the doubts that have plagued your mind. But know this—you are not alone. You are part of something greater than yourself, woven into the very fabric of existence."

Tears welled in Allie's eyes as she listened to the figure's words, a sense of belonging washing over her like a gentle tide. For the first time in her life, she felt truly seen and understood, accepted for who she was in all her imperfect glory.

With a sense of reverence, Allie knelt before the figure, her heart overflowing with gratitude and awe. In that moment, she knew that her journey was just beginning— that she had found her place in the world and the purpose she had been searching for.

As she rose to her feet, a sense of peace settled over her like a warm embrace. With renewed determination, Allie set out to embrace the path that lay before her, guided by the wisdom of the forest and the knowledge that she was never truly alone.

And as she disappeared into the depths of the forest, a sense of hope and possibility filled the air—a whisper of promise that carried on the wind, echoing through the trees and into the hearts of all who called the forest home.

CHAPTER 15: VALENCIA'S VISION

Valencia stood atop the highest peak in the mountain range that encircled Sommerville, her eyes fixed on the horizon as the sun dipped below the edge of the world. The cool mountain air whispered through her hair, carrying with it the scent of pine and the promise of a new day.

For as long as she could remember, Valencia had been drawn to the mountains—their towering peaks and sweeping vistas filling her with a sense of wonder and awe. But as she stood atop the summit, she felt a stirring deep within her soul—a longing to connect with something greater than herself.

With a sense of purpose burning in her chest, Valencia closed her eyes and opened her mind to the world around her. She felt the energy of the mountains coursing through her veins, filling her with a sense of power and clarity that she had never known before.

In that moment, Valencia felt a presence beside her—a whisper of ancient wisdom that beckoned her forward. She opened her eyes and saw a figure standing before her, cloaked in robes of silver and blue.

"Welcome, Valencia," the figure said, their voice like the gentle rush of a mountain stream. "I have been expecting you."

Valencia's heart soared with a mixture of awe and wonder as she gazed upon the figure before her. There was a familiarity in their presence—a sense of recognition that resonated deep within her being.

"I have watched you from afar, Valencia," the figure continued, their gaze piercing to the core of her soul. "I have seen the strength and resilience you possess, and the untapped potential that lies within you. But know this— you are not defined by your past. You are the architect of your own destiny, capable of shaping the world according to your vision."

Tears welled in Valencia's eyes as she listened to the figure's words, a sense of purpose filling her heart like a raging river. For the first time in her life, she felt truly empowered, liberated from the shackles of doubt and uncertainty that had held her back for so long.

With a sense of determination, Valencia knelt before the figure, her spirit soaring on the wings of possibility. In that moment, she knew that her journey was just beginning—that she had the power to create the future she desired, guided by the wisdom of the mountains and the knowledge that she was capable of achieving anything she set her mind to.

As she rose to her feet, a sense of exhilaration filled her being. With newfound confidence, Valencia set out to embrace the challenges that lay ahead, ready to carve her own path through the world and leave her mark on the world around her.

And as she disappeared into the fading light of dusk, a sense of anticipation filled the air—a whisper of promise that carried on the wind, echoing through the mountains and into the hearts of all who called them home.

CHAPTER 16: ALLIE'S AWAKENING

In the heart of Sommerville, nestled among the rolling hills and gentle meadows, Allie found herself standing in the midst of a sunlit clearing, surrounded by the vibrant colors of nature in full bloom. The sweet scent of wildflowers filled the air, mingling with the soft rustle of leaves in the breeze.

As Allie gazed around her, she felt a sense of peace wash over her—a quiet calm that settled deep within her soul. For so long, she had been searching for meaning and purpose, lost in the tangled maze of her own thoughts and fears. But in this moment, surrounded by the beauty of the natural world, she felt a glimmer of hope flicker to life within her heart.

With a sense of wonder, Allie reached out to touch the petals of a nearby flower, marveling at the delicate intricacy of its form. As her fingers brushed against the soft petals, she felt a surge of energy course through her—

a connection to something greater than herself, something ancient and timeless.

In that moment, Allie felt as though she were seeing the world through new eyes—a world filled with infinite possibility and boundless potential. She realized that she had been living her life in shades of gray, trapped by her own insecurities and doubts, but now, she saw the world in vibrant technicolor, alive with beauty and wonder.

With each breath she took, Allie felt a sense of clarity wash over her, as though the fog that had clouded her mind for so long had finally lifted. She knew that she had the power to shape her own destiny—to embrace the unknown with courage and determination, and to forge a path forward guided by her own inner light.

As she stood in the clearing, basking in the warmth of the sun and the gentle embrace of the breeze, Allie felt a sense of gratitude well up within her. She was grateful for the journey that had brought her to this moment—for the struggles and challenges that had shaped her into the person she was today.

With a newfound sense of purpose burning in her heart, Allie set out to explore the world around her, eager to discover what wonders lay beyond the confines of her familiar surroundings. She knew that the road ahead would not be easy, but she faced it with a quiet resolve, secure in the knowledge that she was never truly alone.

And as she disappeared into the dappled light of the forest, a sense of anticipation filled the air—a whisper of possibility that carried on the wind, echoing through the trees and into the hearts of all who listened. For Allie, the journey had only just begun, and the future held endless promise and potential for those brave enough to seize it.

CHAPTER 17: VALENCIA'S EQUATION

In the quiet of her classroom, Valencia stood before the whiteboard, her mind buzzing with excitement. She could feel the thrill of discovery coursing through her—a spark of insight waiting to illuminate the mysteries of mathematics.

With a confident hand, Valencia picked up her marker, its ink a promise of the equations yet to come. As she began to write, she felt a sense of clarity descend upon her—a clarity born of logic and reason, guiding her through the labyrinth of numbers and symbols.

With each theorem she proved, Valencia delved deeper into the heart of mathematics, unraveling its secrets with precision and skill. She worked with passion and purpose, allowing her intuition to guide her as she navigated the complexities of the subject.

As the class progressed, Valencia lost herself in the beauty of mathematics, the outside world fading away until all that remained was the rhythm of numbers dancing before her—a symphony of logic and order.

With each problem she solved, Valencia felt a sense of satisfaction wash over her—a satisfaction that came from mastering a discipline as ancient as time itself. She knew that her journey as a mathematician was just beginning, but she faced the future with a newfound confidence and determination.

With a sense of purpose burning in her heart, Valencia set out to share her love of mathematics with her students—to inspire them with the beauty of numbers and the elegance of proofs. She knew that the road ahead would not be easy, but she faced it with courage and conviction, secure in the knowledge that she was following her true calling.

And as she gazed upon the equations before her, Valencia knew that her passion for mathematics would serve as a guiding light for all who sought to understand—

to unlock the secrets of the universe and discover the hidden patterns that connected us all.

73

CHAPTER 18: ALLIE'S CANVAS

In the quiet sanctuary of her studio, Allie stood before a blank canvas, her brushes poised to bring life to the stark whiteness before her. The soft glow of the afternoon sun filtered through the windows, casting a warm embrace over the room as she prepared to embark on her next masterpiece.

With a gentle stroke, Allie began to paint—a delicate dance of color and light unfolding beneath her skilled hand. She worked with passion and purpose, allowing her creativity to flow freely as she brought her vision to life on the canvas.

As the painting took shape, Allie lost herself in the process, the world around her fading away until all that remained was the vibrant tapestry of colors blooming before her—a testament to her talent and imagination.

With each brushstroke, Allie poured her heart and soul into the canvas, channeling her emotions into every stroke and swirl. She painted with an intensity that bordered on obsession, driven by a desire to capture the essence of beauty and truth in its purest form.

As the hours passed, Allie's painting began to evolve— a living, breathing reflection of her innermost thoughts and feelings. She worked tirelessly, pushing herself to new heights as she explored the boundaries of her creativity and skill.

With each layer of paint, Allie's vision grew clearer, her confidence soaring as she transformed the blank canvas into a work of art that spoke to the soul. She knew that her journey as an artist was just beginning, but she faced the future with a sense of excitement and anticipation, eager to see where her talents would take her next.

And as she gazed upon the masterpiece before her, Allie knew that her passion for painting would serve as a beacon of inspiration for all who beheld it—to ignite the spark of creativity within their hearts and inspire them to

chase their dreams with unwavering determination and
joy.

CHAPTER 19: MARY'S REFLECTION

In the quiet corners of Sommerville, Mary found herself lost in a moment of reflection—a chance to ponder the path that had led her to this place and the dreams that had guided her along the way. As she sat beneath the shade of an ancient oak tree, the gentle rustle of the leaves overhead provided a soothing backdrop to her thoughts.

Mary had always been a dreamer—a seeker of beauty and truth in the world around her. From a young age, she had been drawn to the arts, finding solace and inspiration in the colors of the canvas and the melodies of the piano. But as she grew older, she had begun to question whether her dreams were truly attainable, whether the world had a place for a dreamer like her.

It wasn't until she returned to Sommerville, her hometown, that Mary began to see the world with new eyes. Here, amidst the rolling hills and quiet streets, she found a community that embraced her for who she was—

a community that nurtured her dreams and encouraged her to pursue her passions with unwavering determination.

As Mary looked back on her journey, she realized that Sommerville had been more than just a place to call home—it had been a source of inspiration and strength, a wellspring of creativity and possibility. Here, she had found the courage to pursue her dreams, to embrace her true self, and to believe in the power of her own voice.

And so, as the sun dipped below the horizon and the stars began to twinkle overhead, Mary made a silent vow to herself—to never stop dreaming, to never stop believing in the beauty of her own imagination. For she knew that as long as she had Sommerville by her side, she would always have a place to call home, a community to lift her up, and a world of endless possibilities waiting to be explored.

With a renewed sense of purpose and determination, Mary rose to her feet, her heart full of gratitude for the journey that had brought her to this moment. And as she set forth into the night, guided by the light of her dreams and the warmth of her community, she knew that the best was yet to come—a future filled with hope, possibility, and the boundless potential of the human spirit.

CHAPTER 20: SHEILA'S PROMISE

In the quiet moments between the chaos of daily life, Sheila found herself reflecting on the journey that had brought her to this point—a journey marked by trials and triumphs, setbacks and successes. As she sat on the porch of her childhood home, the gentle breeze stirring the leaves overhead, she couldn't help but marvel at how far she had come.

Sheila had always been a fighter—a beacon of strength and resilience in the face of adversity. From a young age, she had faced her fair share of challenges, but she had never let them define her. Instead, she had forged ahead with unwavering determination, fueled by a fierce desire to make a difference in the world.

It wasn't until she returned to Sommerville, her hometown, that Sheila truly found her calling. Here, amidst the familiar streets and familiar faces, she discovered a sense of purpose and belonging that had eluded her for so long. Here, she found a community that embraced her for who she was—a community that saw her potential and encouraged her to chase her dreams with all her heart.

As Sheila looked back on her journey, she realized that Sommerville had been more than just a place to call home—it had been a crucible of transformation, a proving ground where she had honed her skills and discovered her true strength. Here, she had learned to stand tall in the face of adversity, to speak up for those who couldn't speak for themselves, and to fight for justice and equality with every fiber of her being.

And so, as the stars twinkled overhead and the world fell into a peaceful slumber, Sheila made a silent vow to herself—to never stop fighting, to never stop striving for a better tomorrow. For she knew that as long as she had Sommerville by her side, she would always have a home, a community, and a family to support her through whatever challenges lay ahead.

With a sense of purpose burning bright in her heart, Sheila rose to her feet, ready to face whatever the future might bring. And as she gazed out into the night, she knew that the journey was far from over—that the best was yet to come, and that she would face it with courage, determination, and an unwavering belief in the power of community.

CHAPTER 21: JONATHAN'S RESOLVE

In the stillness of the night, Jonathan found himself lost in thought—a lone figure standing on the quiet streets of Sommerville, his mind awash with memories of the past and dreams of the future. As he gazed up at the twinkling stars overhead, he couldn't help but feel a sense of awe at the journey that had brought him to this moment.

Jonathan had always been a seeker—a man driven by a relentless pursuit of truth and justice. From a young age, he had been drawn to the complexities of the world around him, eager to uncover the secrets that lay hidden beneath the surface. But it wasn't until he returned to Sommerville, his hometown, that he truly found his purpose.

Here, amidst the familiar sights and sounds of his youth, Jonathan discovered a sense of belonging that he had never known before. Here, he found a community that welcomed him with open arms—a community that saw his potential and encouraged him to chase his dreams with all his heart.

As Jonathan looked back on his journey, he realized that Sommerville had been more than just a place to call home—it had been a crucible of transformation, a forge where he had been tempered and tested, shaped into the man he was meant to be. Here, he had learned to stand tall in the face of adversity, to fight for what was right, and to never waver in his commitment to justice and truth.

And so, as the moon cast its silver glow over the sleeping town, Jonathan made a silent vow to himself—to never stop seeking, to never stop fighting for what he believed in. For he knew that as long as he had Sommerville by his side, he would always have a home, a community, and a purpose to guide him through the darkest of times.

With a sense of determination burning bright in his heart, Jonathan turned and walked back towards his home, ready to face whatever challenges the future might hold. And as he disappeared into the night, he knew that the journey was far from over—that the best was yet to come, and that he would face it with courage, integrity, and an unwavering belief in the power of community.

CHAPTER 22: EMBRACING THE JOURNEY

As the sun rose on Sommerville, casting its golden light over the town and its residents, there was a palpable sense of peace and renewal in the air. The storm had passed, leaving behind a landscape transformed by its fury—but amidst the wreckage, there was also a sense of hope and possibility, a reminder that even in the darkest of times, there was always light to be found.

For the people of Sommerville, the journey had been long and arduous, marked by trials and tribulations, setbacks and successes. But through it all, they had stood together, united by a common purpose and a shared commitment to their community. And as they looked out at the town they called home, they knew that their journey was far from over—that the road ahead would be filled with new challenges and opportunities, twists and turns, highs and lows.

But they were ready.

Ready to face whatever the future might bring with courage and determination, guided by the lessons they had learned and the bonds they had forged along the way. Ready to rebuild and restore their beloved town to its former glory, one brick at a time. Ready to embrace the journey, wherever it might lead, with open hearts and unwavering faith in the power of community.

As they stood together on the steps of the community center, the heart of Sommerville, they made a silent vow to themselves and to each other—to never stop striving, to never stop fighting for what they believed in. For they knew that as long as they had each other, they would always have hope, strength, and resilience to see them through even the darkest of days.

And so, as they turned to face the future, they did so with heads held high and hearts full of gratitude—for the journey they had shared, for the challenges they had overcome, and for the boundless possibilities that lay ahead.

For Sommerville was more than just a town—it was a community, a family, a home. And together, they would weather any storm and emerge stronger on the other side, guided by the light of their shared dreams and aspirations.

As the people of Sommerville set out to embrace the journey that lay ahead, they knew that their story was just beginning—that the best was yet to come, and that with courage, resilience, and unwavering faith in each other, they could overcome any obstacle and build a future filled with hope, joy, and endless possibility.

ABOUT THE AUTHOR

Gloria Foster is an accomplished author known for her captivating storytelling and ability to delve into the depths of human experiences. With a keen eye for detail and a passion for exploring the complexities of the human psyche, she weaves narratives that both entertain and provoke thought.

Her debut novel, *The Mind*, introduced readers to a cast of unforgettable characters, captivating them with its compelling storyline and thought-provoking themes. It was received with critical acclaim, earning a coveted 5-star review from Readers' Favorite, a testament to Gloria's skill in crafting engaging narratives.

Continuing the journey of her characters, Gloria's second novel, *The Core*, takes readers on an exhilarating ride, blending unexpected twists with a touch of magic. As part of "The Women's Soul" series, *The Core* expands the world established in its predecessor, introducing new characters and delving deeper into the rich tapestry of interconnected lives.

Emerge: A Symphony of Resilience, the final book in this sequel, concludes this compelling series with a powerful exploration of resilience and human spirit.

Gloria's writing has garnered recognition beyond literary circles. Her screenplay adaptation of *The Mind* was honored as a 2021 Screenplay Award Finalist in the prestigious Page Turner Awards, further solidifying her talent as a versatile storyteller.

With a diverse educational background, Gloria holds a Bachelor of Arts degree in Mathematical Sciences from the University of Illinois at Springfield. In addition to her literary pursuits, Gloria maintains an active online presence through her author website at www.gloriafoster.com. Through her website, readers can connect with her, explore her latest projects, and stay updated on future releases.

As an author, Gloria Foster's passion lies in crafting narratives that resonate with readers, exploring the human condition, and shedding light on the complexities of the world we inhabit. With each new work, she invites readers to embark on profound journeys of self-discovery and connection.

The Roots of Violence stands as a testament to Gloria's dedication to her craft, as she fearlessly tackles the intricate dynamics of violence and advocates for positive change in our society. Through her writing, she challenges readers to examine their own beliefs and become catalysts for a more compassionate and just world.

Gloria Foster is an author to watch, as her powerful storytelling continues to captivate readers and ignite conversations that transcend the pages of her books. With a commitment to authenticity and a talent for crafting engaging narratives, she has established herself as a rising star in the literary world.

www.ingramcontent.com/pod-product-compliance
Lightning Source LLC
Chambersburg PA
CBHW071203300726
48975CB00004B/1263